The Ugly D

Retold by Marc A. Cerasini
Illustrated by Michelle Lash-Ruff

©1996 McClanahan Book Company, Inc.
All rights reserved.
Published by McClanahan Book Company, Inc.
23 West 26th Street, New York, NY 10010.
LCC: 96-75638.
Printed in the USA.

In a snug nest in a cozy corner of a little pond, Mamma Duck tended her eggs.

Night and day she kept watch. And every morning she counted the eggs. One, two, three, four.

Then, one sunny morning, Mamma Duck heard a crack. She jumped up from her nest.

Her eggs were hatching, one by one!

Mamma Duck quacked with pride and flapped her wings.

There they were. Three little yellow ducklings, poking their beaks out of their shells.

"Peep! Peep! Peep!" the ducklings cried. They were hungry!

One little egg did not hatch.

"You are not like the others," said Mamma Duck worriedly.
"Why haven't you hatched?"

Then, with a loud crack, the last egg broke open.

"What a strange one! You are not at all like the others,"
Mamma Duck said again.

"Your feathers are not yellow, but brown. Your beak is not
orange, but gray."

"Honk! Honk!" cried the strange little baby.

"You are not like the others!" said Mamma Duck once more.
Gently, she stroked her newest child. "You are my little
Ugly Duckling."

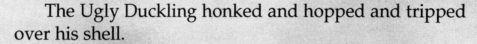

The Ugly Duckling honked and hopped and tripped
over his shell.

"You are not like the others, and you are clumsy, too!"
Mamma Duck said, with a gentle laugh.

"Now, let's see if you can swim like your brothers."

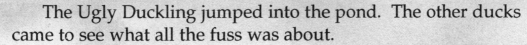

The Ugly Duckling jumped into the pond. The other ducks came to see what all the fuss was about.

"My," said the other ducks, "you are an ugly duckling!"

"But why am I so ugly?" the Ugly Duckling asked.

Sadly, the Ugly Duckling swam away, his head
hanging down.

"Why am I so ugly?" the Ugly Duckling asked his
reflection in the pond.

But the pond had no answer.

"I am so ugly, I can't go home," said the Ugly Duckling. "So, I will find a place in this pond, and make it my own!"

The Ugly Duckling swam and swam, until he reached the far side of the pond.

There he saw a turtle stick his head out of his shell. "I am told that I am ugly," he said, "but so are you."

The turtle nodded his wrinkled brown head.

"We turtles may be ugly, but we are wise."

The Ugly Duckling saw beautiful swans fly across the sky.
He saw their long, white necks and strong, white wings.
"I wish I could be beautiful like they are," the Ugly
Duckling said.
"But I am too ugly! Everybody says so!"

The Ugly Duckling found a safe place on the shore. He hid in the tall grass and covered his face with one wing.

The nights grew cold and the days became short.

The winter wind whistled around the Ugly Duckling.

"Why am I so ugly?" the Ugly Duckling asked the wind as it blew and blew.

"Who knows?" answered the wind.

The winter was long, but finally spring came. The sun
warmed the pond.
And a strange thing happened.
The Ugly Duckling began to grow . . . and grow . . . and grow!

His neck grew long and his brown feathers turned as white as the winter snow.

But the Ugly Duckling still hid himself in the tall grass.

One sunny day, the Ugly Duckling spread his wings and something wonderful happened.

Up, up he went.

"Look at me! I can fly!" cried the Ugly Duckling.

"Look! Look at him!" cried the ducks below.

The Ugly Duckling landed in the pond with a splash. The ducks were waiting for him.

"Look! Look at you!" they said. "From the tips of your wings to your neck and beak, too!"

"Yes, I know," said the Ugly Duckling, ashamed. He hung his head low. But when he saw his reflection, he honked in surprise.

There was no Ugly Duckling there at all, but the most beautiful creature in the entire pond!
"Oh my," he said. "Is that me?"
"Yes!" said the ducks. "That's you!"

The Ugly Duckling saw the wise
old turtle crawling up onto the shore.
    "Tell me turtle, tell me true, am
I beautiful?"
    "Beautiful, yes!" the turtle said.

"If you had asked me before, I could have told you that you would be beautiful. You see, my little Ugly Duckling, you have turned into a swan."

The swans gathered around the Ugly Duckling.
"You are one of us," they said.
"Come, let's swim away together."

And so they swam across the water, all of them beautiful, graceful, and strong. And the Ugly Duckling, who was no longer ugly, held his head high and spread his wings against the wind.